A NOTE TO PARENTS

When your children are ready to "step into reading," giving them the right books—and lots of them—is as crucial as giving them the right food to eat. **Step into Reading Books** present exciting stories and information reinforced with lively, colorful illustrations that make learning to read fun, satisfying, and worthwhile. They are priced so that acquiring an entire library of them is affordable. And they are beginning readers with an important difference—they're written on four levels.

Step 1 Books, with their very large type and extremely simple vocabulary, have been created for the very youngest readers. **Step 2 Books** are both longer and slightly more difficult. **Step 3 Books,** written to mid-second-grade reading levels, are for the child who has acquired even greater reading skills. **Step 4 Books** offer exciting nonfiction for the increasingly proficient reader.

Children develop at different ages. **Step into Reading Books,** with their four levels of reading, are designed to help children become good—and interested—readers *faster*. The grade levels assigned to the four steps—preschool through grade 1 for Step 1, grades 1 through 3 for Step 2, grades 2 and 3 for Step 3, and grades 2 through 4 for Step 4—are intended only as guides. Some children move through all four steps very rapidly; others climb the steps over a period of several years. These books will help your child "step into reading" in style!

In memory of my father, Samuel J. Margolin   —H.Z.

Text copyright © 1985 by Harriet Ziefert. Illustrations copyright © 1985 by Carol Nicklaus. All rights reserved under International and Pan-American Copyright Conventions. Published in the United States by Random House, Inc., New York, and simultaneously in Canada by Random House of Canada Limited, Toronto.

Library of Congress Cataloging in Publication Data:
Ziefert, Harriet. A dozen dogs. (Step into reading. A Step 1 book) SUMMARY: A dozen dogs frolicking on the beach introduce the numbers one through twelve. 1. Counting—Juvenile literature. [1. Counting. 2. Dogs—Fiction] I. Nicklaus, Carol, ill. II. Title. III. Series: Step into reading book. Step 1 book. QA113.Z54 1985 513'.2 [E] 84-17797 ISBN: 0-394-86935-4 (trade); 0-394-96935-9 (lib. bdg.)

Manufactured in the United States of America   24 25 26 27 28 29 30

STEP INTO READING is a trademark of Random House, Inc.

Step into Reading™

A DOZEN DOGS

A Read-and-Count Story

by Harriet Ziefert
illustrated by Carol Nicklaus

A Step 1 Book

Random House 🏠 New York

Chapter 1: A Dozen Dogs

Two dogs going to the beach.

Want to come along?

One fat dog.

One skinny dog.

One white dog.

One black dog.

One black and white dog.

Five dogs going to the beach.

Two brown dogs—

they look like twins!

Three hungry puppies—
they like hot dogs!

Another five dogs
going to the beach.

1, 2, 3, 4, 5, 6, 7, 8, 9, 10, 11, 12 . . .
Twelve dogs at the beach.

Dogs meet dogs.

Dogs greet dogs.

Yakety-yak!

A dozen dogs.

Chapter 2: Swimming

A dozen dogs on a raft.

They want to go swimming.

Want to come along?

Five dogs dive.

Splash!

Seven dogs on a raft.

Five dogs jump.
Splash!

Now just two dogs on a raft.

Ten barking dogs in the water.

"Jump in, bow-wow!

Jump in, right now!"

Two dogs on a raft
too scared to jump.

What can they do?

They can jump together.

1, 2, 3 . . . JUMP!

No dogs on a raft.

A dozen dogs going swimming.
See them do the doggy-paddle!

Chapter 3: Fishing

Two dogs going fishing.

Want to come along?

Two dogs in a boat
catching fish.
One big fish.
One little fish.

One spotted fish.

One dotted fish.

Two dogs catch four fish.

Two dogs in a boat
catching fish.
One fat fish.
One skinny fish.

Two red fish . . . twins!

Two dogs catch four more fish.

1, 2, 3, 4, 5, 6, 7, 8 . . .

Eight fish!

Two dogs in a boat catching . . .

A WHALE!

Two dogs going swimming.
Want to come along?